A Note to Parents and Caregivers:

Read-it! Readers are for children who are just starting on the amazing road to reading. These beautiful books support both the acquisition of reading skills and the love of books.

 The PURPLE LEVEL presents basic topics and objects using high frequency words and simple language patterns.

 The RED LEVEL presents familiar topics using common words and repeating sentence patterns.

 The BLUE LEVEL presents new ideas using a larger vocabulary and varied sentence structure.

 The YELLOW LEVEL presents more challenging ideas, a broad vocabulary, and wide variety in sentence structure.

 The GREEN LEVEL presents more complex ideas, an extended vocabulary range, and expanded language structures.

 The ORANGE LEVEL presents a wide range of ideas and concepts using challenging vocabulary and complex language structures.

When sharing a book with your child, read in short stretches, pausing often to talk about the pictures. Have your child turn the pages and point to the pictures and familiar words. And be sure to reread favorite stories or parts of stories.

There is no right or wrong way to share books with children. Find time to read with your child, and pass on the legacy of literacy.

Adria F. Klein, Ph.D.
Professor Emeritus
California State University
San Bernardino, California

Editor: Jill Kalz
Designer: Tracy Davies
Page Production: Melissa Kes
Art Director: Nathan Gassman
Associate Managing Editor: Christianne Jones
The illustrations in this book were created with watercolor.

Picture Window Books
5115 Excelsior Boulevard
Suite 232
Minneapolis, MN 55416
877-845-8392
www.picturewindowbooks.com

Printed in the United States of America.

Library of Congress Cataloging-in-Publication Data
Shaskan, Trisha Speed, 1973–
Camden's game / by Trisha Speed Shaskan ; illustrated by Necdet Yilmaz.
p. cm. — (Read-it! readers)
Summary: Camden loves to play basketball with his mother, and while he plays he
wonders if he dribbles better than an ostrich, runs faster than a cheetah, or jumps as
high as a frog.
ISBN-13: 978-1-4048-3136-0 (library binding)
ISBN-10: 1-4048-3136-3 (library binding)
ISBN-13: 978-1-4048-1226-0 (paperback)
ISBN-10: 1-4048-1226-1 (paperback)
[1. Basketball—Fiction. 2. Mothers and sons—Fiction. 3. English language—
Comparison—Fiction.] I. Yilmaz, Necdet, 1970– ill. II. Title.
PZ7.S53242Cam 2006
[E]—dc22
2006027282

Camden's Game

by Trisha Speed Shaskan
illustrated by Necdet Yilmaz

Special thanks to our advisers for their expertise:

Adria F. Klein, Ph.D.
Professor Emeritus, California State University
San Bernardino, California

Susan Kesselring, M.A.
Literacy Educator
Rosemount–Apple Valley–Eagan (Minnesota) School District

PiCTURE WiNDOW BOOKS
Minneapolis, Minnesota

My name is Camden, and basketball is my favorite sport. My mom and I play a lot. I even do tricks.

I spin the ball on my finger and say, "Mom, if I were a seal, I would spin the ball on my nose."

"I suppose you would," Mom says.

5

When I move down the court, I dribble the ball behind my right knee, then my left. I wonder, what if I were an ostrich?

If I were an ostrich, my legs would be long and skinny. I could slip the ball easily between them.

When I move across the court, I go fast.
I wonder, what if I were a cheetah?

If I were a cheetah, I would run so fast that my spots would blur. Nobody could catch me!

I put my arm out to protect the ball. I wonder, what if I were an octopus?

If I were an octopus, I would have eight arms. Nobody could steal the ball from me!

When I start to shoot the ball, I bend my knees. Then I leap into the air. I wonder, what if I were a frog?

If I were a frog, my legs would bend like rubber bands. I could jump off the court as if it were a trampoline.

When I let go of the ball, it soars toward the hoop. I wonder, what if I were a pelican?

If I were a pelican, I would carry the ball in my bill and fly through the air. No one could reach me!

My shot bounces off the backboard. It rolls around the rim. I wonder, what if I were a monkey?

If I were a monkey, I would climb the pole, tap the ball into the hoop, and hang onto the rim. My hang time would break records!

When Mom's shot misses the hoop, she and I jump for the rebound. I wonder, what if I were a kangaroo?

If I were a kangaroo, I would jump up and catch the ball in my pouch. The ball would be safe there.

Mom catches the rebound, and I guard her.
I wonder, what if I were a rhinoceros?

If I were a rhinoceros, I would stand guard with my horn raised in the air. It would be hard to dribble around me.

But if I were any of those animals, I couldn't play with my mom.

I'm glad I'm Camden. And Mom is glad, too!

More *Read-it!* Readers

Bright pictures and fun stories help you practice your reading skills. Look for more books at your level.

Alex and Toolie
Another Pet
The Big Pig
Bliss, Blueberries, and the Butterfly
Cass the Monkey
Charlie's Tasks
Clever Cat
Flora McQuack
Kyle's Recess
Marconi the Wizard
Peppy, Patch, and the Postman
Peter's Secret
Pets on Vacation
The Princess and the Tower
Theodore the Millipede
The Three Princesses
Tromso the Troll
Willie the Whale
The Zoo Band

Looking for a specific title or level? A complete list of *Read-it!* Readers is available on our Web site:
www.picturewindowbooks.com